This book belongs to:

_____

_____

_____

Published by Greenleaf Book Group Press
Austin, Texas
www.gbgpress.com

Distributed by Greenleaf Book Group

For ordering information or special discounts for bulk purchases, please contact Greenleaf Book Group at PO Box 91869, Austin, TX 78709, 512.891.6100.

Design and composition by Greenleaf Book Group
Cover design by Greenleaf Book Group

Publisher's Cataloging-in-Publication data is available.

Print ISBN: 978-1-62634-771-7
eBook ISBN: 978-1-62634-772-4

Part of the Tree Neutral® program, which offsets the number of trees consumed in the production and printing of this book by taking proactive steps, such as planting trees in direct proportion to the number of trees used: www.treeneutral.com

Manufactured through Asia Pacific Offset on acid-free paper
Manufactured in China on September 2021
Batch number: Q21050079

21 22 23 24 25 26   10 9 8 7 6 5 4 3 2 1

First Edition

Lulu

the Unstoppable Dancing Dog

Marie Dimitrova

ILLUSTRATED BY Romi Caron

GREENLEAF
BOOK GROUP PRESS

How many dog bones can you find hidden throughout the story?

Lulu the pug lived in New York City with the beautiful Belle and the dashing Doug. The three of them did everything together.

They enjoyed all of the wonderful things
their beautiful city had to offer, such as

walking in Central Park,

visiting museums,

and seeing Broadway shows.

One of their favorite things to do together was eat all the yummy food
New York City had to offer. Their favorite place to eat was Joey's Pizza. And
every time they would go, Lulu would bark and chase her tail with excitement.

The only thing Lulu loved more than eating pizza was going with Belle and Doug to their dance lessons. Each week, she watched as they gracefully waltzed across the floor.

Look at them spin.

Look at them turn.

Look at them sashay! she thought. *I want to do that, too!*

Night after night, while Belle and Doug slept,
Lulu tried to imitate their waltz.

One day, at Belle and Doug's dance lesson, Lulu got so excited she couldn't
sit still any longer. She wanted to dance, too, so she ran onto the dance floor.
She hopped around on her back legs, trying to waltz like Belle and Doug.

"Ms. Harriet," Belle said to her dance instructor. "I think Lulu is trying to waltz!"

"That's ridiculous," Ms. Harriet said, laughing meanly. "Dogs can't dance!"

Lulu became angry. *I'll show Ms. Harriet that dogs can dance, too!* she thought to herself.

Belle bent to give Lulu a hug. "It's okay, Lulu. You tried your best. How about we go get some pizza at Joey's?"

Lulu followed Belle and Doug to Joey's Pizza. But for the first time, her heart wasn't in the meal. All she could think about was learning to waltz.

On the way home, Lulu saw something that changed her mood:
A pug stood on his hind legs, his paws and body moving
effortlessly through the air. He was waltzing!

"Excuse me, sir, but you are a marvelous dancer!
Can you teach me how to move like that?" asked Lulu.

"Why, I would love to! My name is Stu,"
said the dancing pug.

"Nice to meet you, Stu!
My name is Lulu."

"A pleasure, Lulu. Meet me tomorrow at three o'clock at the Underground Dog Dance Academy. It's hidden down the alleyway next to Joey's Pizza."

"I will!" said Lulu. "I can't wait!"

"Good," said Stu. "And Lulu—be ready to learn how to waltz!"

The next day, while Belle and Doug were at work, Lulu snuck out using the fire escape and went to meet Stu at the Underground Dog Dance Academy.

At her first lesson, Lulu learned the basic steps.

The next day, Lulu returned.
And the day after that, and
the day after that.

Slowly but surely, Lulu became better and better.

She learned
proper posture

and how to spin,

and she even learned how to sashay.

Lulu knew that Belle and Doug had a recital coming up, and she wanted to show them what she had learned.
"If you keep practicing, I think you'll be ready," Stu encouraged her. "I'll come dance with you, and we'll show everybody that dogs can waltz, too!"

Excited, Lulu headed home to practice. *I really want to get better at waltzing so I can dance with Belle and Doug,* she thought.

But on her way home, as she passed Joey's Pizza, Lulu became distracted.
She forgot about practicing and instead stopped for a slice of pizza.
Each day, after her lesson, she stopped for pizza rather than practicing.

A few days later, Lulu went with Belle and Doug to their dance recital. Stu was already there, waiting to dance with Lulu.

Lulu was excited to surprise Belle and Doug with her new moves.

But when she and Stu took the stage, Lulu froze.

She forgot her waltz. Lulu had not practiced enough.

She slouched and tripped on her spin.

She even fell in her sashay.

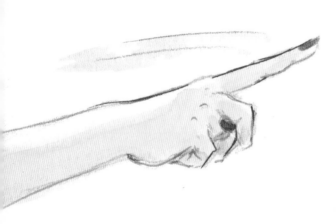

"Is Lulu trying to waltz again?" Belle asked Doug.

"See, dogs can't waltz!" said Ms. Harriet.

Embarrassed, Lulu ran off the stage.

"What happened, Lulu?" Stu asked.
"I thought you were practicing at home . . ."

"I'm sorry!" Lulu said in a nervous voice.
"I was going to, but then I would pass
Joey's Pizza each day, and I couldn't help myself!"

"So instead of practicing,
you were eating pizza?" asked Stu.

Lulu put her head down. "Yes," she said.

"I understand," Stu told her, placing his paw on her shoulder. "There is another show coming up soon! It's the biggest show of the year—the one and only Grand Ballroom Showcase! If you will practice, I think you can compete, but you can't get distracted by pizza."

"I know," Lulu said. "I'll do better, I promise. I'll practice and show everyone that I can waltz, too!"

For the next few weeks, Lulu met with Stu whenever she could.

And every night, when Belle and Doug were sleeping, she practiced her dance moves.

Day after day, she worked hard. And pretty soon, Lulu could fly across the dance floor with ease.

She even sashayed across the floor beautifully.

She held her body gracefully and spun around elegantly.

Finally, the big day arrived. Lulu went with Belle and Doug to the competition—little did they know that Lulu intended to enter, too.

"Welcome to the Grand Ballroom Showcase!" said the announcer. Soft music played as dancers glided across the floor.

"Let's show everybody that you can waltz, too!" Stu said, and, grabbing Lulu by the paw, the two waltzed gracefully across the floor, just like they had practiced.

"Wow, she's incredible! Unbelievable!" Doug said.

Everything was going great, until suddenly, Lulu smelled a familiar scent. Her eyes locked on a little girl in the crowd eating Joey's pizza.

She paused for a second . . .

But then she heard an amazing sound: "Lulu! Lulu! Lulu!"
It was Belle and Doug cheering her on.

Lulu sashayed
right next to
the girl, and . . .

. . . continued her waltz flawlessly!

She spun gracefully
and twirled effortlessly.

Lulu pranced around
the floor with confidence.

Lulu waltzed like she had never waltzed before.

When the dance was over, she and
Stu bowed deeply, and the
audience cheered wildly.

After all the couples had danced, the contestants stood together, waiting to hear who had won.

Lulu and Stu stood beside Belle and Doug. Lulu was proud of herself and happy to have finally shown off her skills.

"And the winners are . . ." the announcer said at last.

The audience waited in suspense.

"Breaking ballroom dance history—our doggy dancers, Lulu and Stu!
The first dogs to ever win the Grand Ballroom Showcase!" said the announcer.

"We did it, Lulu!" said Stu, giving her a hug.
"I can't wait to tell everyone at the
Underground Dog Dance Academy
the good news!"

Just then, Ms. Harriet, who had been
watching the whole time, walked up to Lulu.

"Well, you proved me wrong,"
Ms. Harriet told Lulu. "I never
knew dogs could waltz!"

"Who knew Lulu could waltz? She might even be better than us!" said Doug to Belle.

Belle grinned and patted Lulu on the head. "I knew it all along. I'm proud of you, Lulu. Looks like you'll be waltzing with us from now on."

"I suppose I was wrong to judge so quickly. With practice and determination, anything is possible," said Ms. Harriet. "Congratulations, Lulu! How about we all go get some pizza to celebrate? My treat!"

1st
~PLACE~
AWARDED TO
Lulu & Stu

And so, with the biggest smile,
Lulu sashayed and twirled out the door.

Let's Draw Lulu!

1. 2. 3. 4. 5.

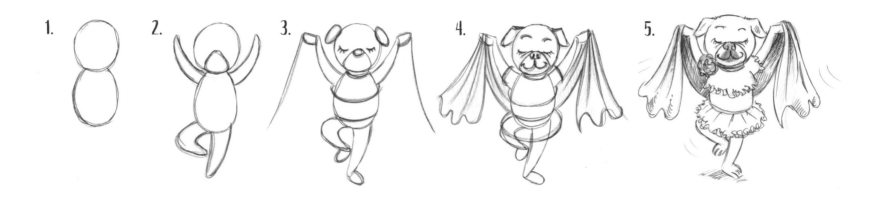

1. 2. 3.

4.

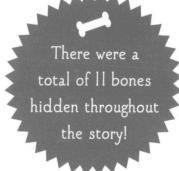

There were a total of 11 bones hidden throughout the story!

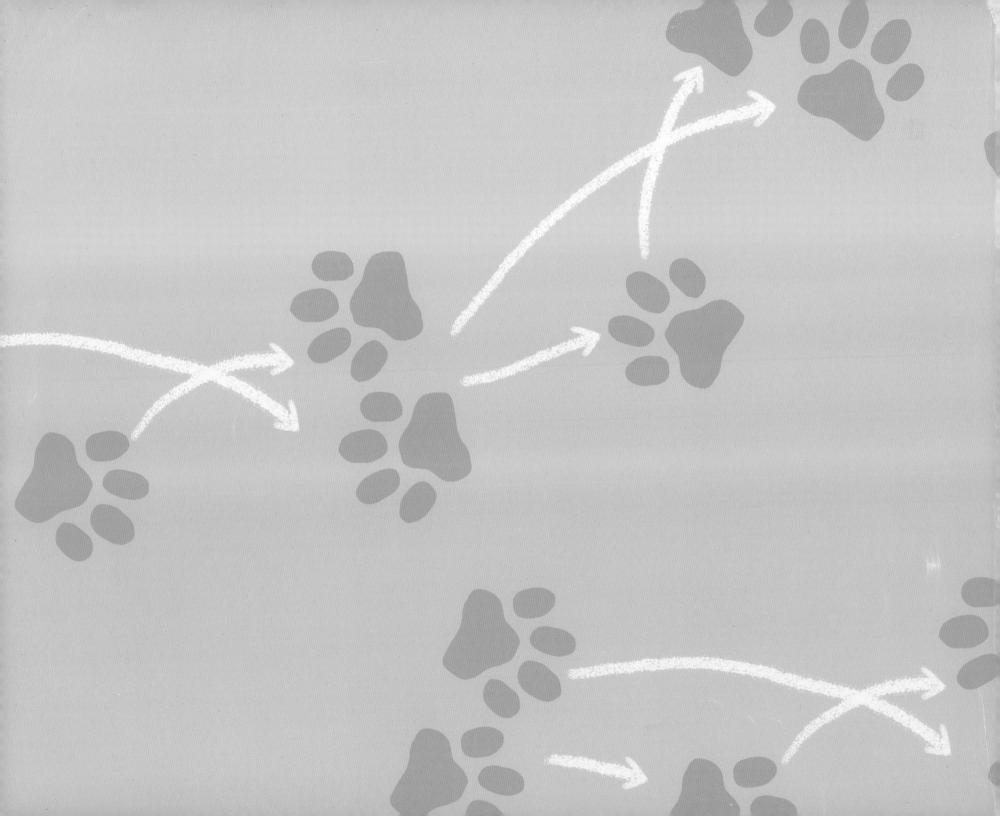